The Clever Kitten

Poor Cosy the kitten! She can't be the nursery kitten anymore, but must go downstairs and be the kitchen cat!

Enid Blyton's

The Clever Kitten

Cosy was a little tabby kitten, five months old. She was called Cosy because she always looked such a cosy bundle when she curled herself up on a cushion.

She lived upstairs in the nursery, and the children made a great fuss of her. But Mother said she must soon be a kitchen cat and go and catch mice in the larder.

The children were upset. They did so love having Cosy in the nursery. Sometimes she slept in the doll's cot, and often she went out for a walk wheeled in the doll's pram.

"Mother! If you make her live in the kitchen she will grow fat and lazy and won't play any more!" said Lucy. "Oh, please, do let her belong to us and be the nursery cat."

But Mother didn't seem to think it would be a good idea at all. So Cosy was told that for one week more she could be a nursery kitten—and then she must go downstairs and become a kitchen cat.

Now one afternoon Cosy had a shock. She was sitting upstairs in the nursery armchair, dozing, wondering if she should get up and try and catch a fly that was buzzing round the table, when she suddenly saw somebody looking right in through the window.

Cosy jumped and spat. She arched her little striped back and hissed at the face that looked in at the window. She knew who it was. It was the garden boy, Alfred, who had sometimes caught her and pulled her tail. And now here was Alfred staring in at the nursery window. Whatever was he there for?

The nursery was upstairs. Cosy wondered if Alfred had suddenly grown legs long enough to reach to the nursery. It was most extraordinary. She didn't know that Alfred was standing on a ladder. He had been sent up to tie a big branch of the climbing rose tree that had got loose.

Alfred stared into the nursery. The cupboard door was open, and in the cupboard Alfred saw things that made his mouth water. There was a bag of sugar lumps. A tin of biscuits stood there too. A bottle of sweets was next to it. A slab of chocolate was nearby. Goodness! Alfred thought it was marvellous to see so many good things together.

He looked down into the garden. Nobody was there. He peered carefully into the nursery. Nobody was there either. "I'll chance it!" said Alfred to himself. "I could get all those things into my pocket!"

Now as Alfred climbed in at the window, he pushed the ladder, quite by accident, and it fell to the ground below! And there was Alfred in the nursery, with no ladder to get down again by! He would have to go down the stairs.

Cosy the kitten glared at him. She didn't like the unkind garden boy at all. She spat and hissed at him. He threw a brick at her from the brick box and it hit Cosy on the tail.

The kitten leapt out of the chair and
flew at Alfred. She scratched him down
the hand. Oh, if only, only she could
make someone come and catch this
bad boy before he took all the things
out of the cupboard!

And then Cosy had a marvellous idea! The nursery piano was open. She had often seen Lucy playing on it, making all kinds of noises, deep and loud, and high and tinkly. Perhaps Cosy could make a noise on it too, and then someone might hear and come to the nursery!

So Cosy leapt up on to the open piano and ran up and down the black and white keys. *Ping, ping, pong, dingle-dingle, doom*! went the keys, making a funny little tune of their own.

Cosy was rather frightened. It was funny to make noises with her feet. But she went on and on running up and down the piano, though Alfred threw another brick at her to make her get off!

Now Mother was sitting in the room below, reading. She knew that Nurse and the children were out. And when she heard the strange noise going on upstairs she couldn't *imagine* what it was!

She jumped up and listened. *Ping, ping, pong, dingle, dingle, DOOM*! went the noise. The loud, deep *DOOM* sound was the lowest key on the piano.

"It's someone banging about on the nursery piano!" said Mother, in great astonishment. "Whoever can it be?"

She ran upstairs to see—and when she
got to the nursery, what did she find but
Alfred stuffing his pockets full of sugar
lumps and sweets and biscuits! And
there was Cosy still on the piano,
playing the keys by running up and
down, up and down!

"Alfred!" said Mother. And how Alfred jumped! In two minutes he was downstairs, and the gardener was telling him just exactly what he thought of him, and just what happened to bad boys who climbed in at other people's windows and stole. What a shock for Alfred! How thrilled the children were when they came home and heard all that had happened!

"Clever little Cosy!" cried Lucy, picking up the purring kitten. "Mother, don't make her into a kitchen cat, please, please, don't! Why, she can even play the nursery piano! And she has saved all our biscuits and sweets and sugar. Mother, do let her belong to the nursery always and always!"

"Very well," said Mother, with a laugh. "You can have Cosy for your own. But do teach her to play the piano properly, my dears, because although the noise she made was very good for catching a thief, I wouldn't at all like to hear it going on all day long!"

So Lucy is going to teach Cosy to play the piano properly. Do you think she will be able to?